THIS BOOK
BELONGS TO:

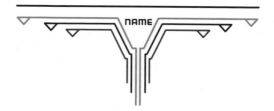

name

How will you practice confidence for the next 365 days?

_____

_____

_____

_____

_____

_____

_____

_____

_____

_____

_____

_____

_____

_____

_____

_____

_____

_____ / _____ / _____

Finish this sentence! I matter because _____.

Write down a positive affirmation for today.

Example: I am powerful.

_____

_____

_____

_____

_____

_____

_____

_____

_____

_____

_____

_____

_____

_____

_____

_____

_____

_____ / _____ / _____

Name three things you did well today.

1

_____

_____

_____

_____

_____

2

_____

_____

_____

_____

3

_____

_____

_____

_____

_____

What do you want to accomplish this week?

_____

_____

_____

_____

_____

_____

_____

_____

_____

_____

_____

_____

_____

_____

_____

_____

_____

_____

_____

_ _ / _ _ / _ _

Try to give at least one meaningful compliment today.
How did others respond?

Time for a check-in! Use this page to describe how you're
feeling physically, mentally, and emotionally.

_____

_____

_____

_____

_____

_____

_____

_____

_____

_____

_____

_____

_____

_____

_____

_____

_____

_____

_____

_____

_____

When faced with a hard decision, T'Challa speaks with his ancestors for guidance. If you had to make a tough choice, which of your ancestors might you turn to?

_____

_____

_____

_____

_____

_____

_____

_____

_____

_____

_____

_____

_____

_____

_____

_____

_____

_____

_____

_____

What advice would you give your younger self?

_ _ / _ _ / _ _

___ / ___ / ___

What does strength mean to you? Describe the many
ways one can show strength.

_____

_____

_____

_____

_____

_____

_____

_____

_____

_____

_____

_____

_____

_____

_____

_____

_____

_____

_____

Draw a time when you felt the most strong, powerful, and free. Who were you with and what were you doing?

___ / ___ / ___

If you had a free ticket to travel anywhere, where would you go and why?

_____

_____

_____

_____

_____

_____

_____

_____

_____

_____

_____

_____

_____

_____

_____

_____

_____

_____

What does community mean to you?

___/___/___

Time for a check-in! **Use this page to describe how you're feeling physically, mentally, and emotionally.**

_____

_____

_____

_____

_____

_____

_____

_____

_____

_____

_____

_____

_____

_____

_____

_____

_____

_____

Goal-setting time! List three new goals for yourself and check back when you finish this journal to see your progress.

1

_____

_____

_____

_____

_____

2

_____

_____

_____

_____

3

_____

_____

_____

_____

_____

_____

_/_/_

In January, we celebrate the birthday of civil rights activist Dr. Martin Luther King Jr. Write down one of his quotes and then write what it means to you.

_____

_____

_____

_____

_____

_____

_____

_____

_____

_____

_____

_____

_____

_____

_____

_____

_____

_____

How can you give back to your community?

Have you seen Marvel Studios's *Black Panther*? What was your favorite part and why?

_____ / _____ / _____

_____

_____

_____

_____

_____

_____

_____

_____

_____

_____

_____

_____

_____

_____

_____

_____

_____

_____

What colors make you feel happy? Draw a fun scene below using those colors.

Reflect on a time that you forgave someone when it was difficult. What did you learn from that experience?

Time for a check-in! **Use this page to describe how you're feeling physically, mentally, and emotionally.**

_ / _ / _

_____

_____

_____

_____

_____

_____

_____

_____

_____

_____

_____

_____

_____

_____

_____

_____

_____

_____

_____

_____

_____

What do you want to learn in the next year?

_____

_____

_____

_____

_____

_____

_____

_____

_____

_____

_____

_____

_____

_____

_____

_____

_____

_____

What would you do if all your fear disappeared?

_____

_____

_____

_____

_____

_____

_____

_____

_____

_____

_____

_____

_____

_____

_____

_____

_____

Who do you go to when you're stressed or frustrated?

Name a character from a movie, book, or TV show that reminds you of yourself.

_____

_____

_____

_____

_____

_____

_____

_____

_____

_____

_____

_____

_____

_____

_____

_____

_____ / _____ / _____

If you were a journalist for your local newspaper, what would you share about your community? Write the opening paragraph of your news story.

_____

_____

_____

_____

_____

_____

_____

_____

_____

_____

_____

_____

_____

_____

_____

_____

_____

_____

_____

_____

What helps you make good decisions?

___ / ___ / ___

Time for a check-in! Use this page to describe how you're feeling physically, mentally, and emotionally.

_____

_____

_____

_____

_____

_____

_____

_____

_____

_____

_____

_____

_____

_____

_____

_____

_____

_____

_____

_____

List three ways you can lead by example.

1

2

3

How can you give joy to others?

_____

_____

_____

_____

_____

_____

_____

_____

_____

_____

_____

_____

_____

_____

_____

_____

_____

_____

Practice speaking with confidence today by standing up straight, making eye contact, and smiling. Write down how that felt.

_____

_____

_____

_____

_____

_____

_____

_____

_____

_____

_____

_____

_____

_____

_____

_____

_____

_____

_ / _ / _

February is Black History Month in the United States. How does learning about history lead to a better future?

Black Panther was the first Black super hero in Marvel comic books, having debuted in 1966. Research another empowering person from the 1960s and write about them here.

_____

_____

_____

_____

_____

_____

_____

_____

_____

_____

_____

_____

_____

_____

_____

_____

_____

_____

_____

_____ / _____ / _____

What does strength look like to you?

_____

_____

_____

_____

_____

_____

_____

_____

_____

_____

_____

_____

_____

_____

_____

_____

_____

_____

_____

Time for a check-in! **Use this page to describe how you're feeling physically, mentally, and emotionally.**

_____

_____

_____

_____

_____

_____

_____

_____

_____

_____

_____

_____

_____

_____

_____

_____

_____

_____

_____

_____

What's your biggest weakness, and how can you turn it into a strength?

_____

_____

_____

_____

_____

_____

_____

_____

_____

_____

_____

_____

_____

_____

_____

_____

_____

List the people who make up your community.

_____ / _____ / _____

_ / _ / _

Finish this sentence! The things that make us unique are our super-powers. What makes me unique is _____ .

What do you love most about yourself? Why?

What are some ways to build trust with the people you care about?

_____

_____

_____

_____

_____

_____

_____

_____

_____

_____

_____

_____

_____

_____

_____

_____

_____

_____

_____

_____

Write about a time that you did something for the first time.

_____ / _____ / _____

_____

_____

_____

_____

_____

_____

_____

_____

_____

_____

_____

_____

_____

_____

_____

_____

_____

_____

___ / ___ / ___

Time for a check-in! **Use this page to describe how you're feeling physically, mentally, and emotionally.**

_____

_____

_____

_____

_____

_____

_____

_____

_____

_____

_____

_____

_____

_____

_____

_____

_____

_____

Think of one skill you want to learn in the next year.
How can you empower yourself to learn something new?

How can you use your power for good? Use an example from movies, books, or even real life.

_____

_____

_____

_____

_____

_____

_____

_____

_____

_____

_____

_____

_____

_____

_____

_____

_____

_____

Does love make you feel strong? Why or why not?

___ / ___ / ___

Goal-setting time! List three new goals and check back when you finish this journal to see your progress.

1 _____
_____
_____
_____
_____

2 _____
_____
_____
_____
_____

3 _____
_____
_____
_____
_____
_____

What advice do you have to give to those who look up to you?

_____

_____

_____

_____

_____

_____

_____

_____

_____

_____

_____

_____

_____

_____

_____

_____

_____

_____

_____

_____/_____/_____

How can you help those who are less fortunate than you are?

Time for a check-in! **Use this page to describe how you're feeling physically, mentally, and emotionally.**

_____

_____

_____

_____

_____

_____

_____

_____

_____

_____

_____

_____

_____

_____

_____

_____

_____

_____

_____

Inventors like Madam C. J. Walker changed the world. Research a new inventor today. What did they invent and why?

_____ / _____ / _____

_____

_____

_____

_____

_____

_____

_____

_____

_____

_____

_____

_____

_____

_____

_____

_____

_____

Why is building community important?

_____ / _____ / _____

Draw yourself as a tall, strong tree. What are the roots of your strength and where does your strength come from?

Research the cultural practices of a community different from your own. Write about what you learn!

_ _/_ _/_ _

_____

_____

_____

_____

_____

_____

_____

_____

_____

_____

_____

_____

_____

_____

_____

_____

_____ / _____ / _____

Reflect on a time when you encouraged someone else.
How did that make you feel?

_____

_____

_____

_____

_____

_____

_____

_____

_____

_____

_____

_____

_____

_____

_____

_____

_____

_____

_____

If you had all the power in the world, how would you use it?

_____ / _____ / _____

Time for a check-in! **Use this page to describe how you're feeling physically, mentally, and emotionally.**

Do you know someone at school who might feel that they don't belong? How can you help them feel included?

_____

_____

_____

_____

_____

_____

_____

_____

_____

_____

_____

_____

_____

_____

_____

_____

_____

_____

__/__/__

Wakandans honor both innovation and tradition. What traditions do your friends or family maintain and value? How might you update those traditions to pass on to future generations?

_____

_____

_____

_____

_____

_____

_____

_____

_____

_____

_____

_____

_____

_____

_____

_____

_____

Where does your power come from?

Replace the last letter in KING for a hint at what makes a great leader. What else makes a queen or king great?

How do you communicate when you are stressed out or frustrated?

_____

_____

_____

_____

_____

_____

_____

_____

_____

_____

_____

_____

_____

_____

_____

_____

_____

_____

_____

_____ / _____ / _____

The Black Panther suit is constantly updated and improved.
Draw your own version and describe its features.

Time for a check-in! **Use this page to describe how you're feeling physically, mentally, and emotionally.**

_____ / _____ / _____

_____

_____

_____

_____

_____

_____

_____

_____

_____

_____

_____

_____

_____

_____

_____

_____

_____

_____

___/___/___

Taking deep breaths is a good way to combat fear.
How else can you relax when you're scared or angry?

If you could write a movie or TV show about any
historical figure, who would you choose and what would
you write about?

_____ / _____ / _____

What activities make you feel proud?

_____

_____

_____

_____

_____

_____

_____

_____

_____

_____

_____

_____

_____

_____

_____

_____

_____

_____

_____

When times get tough, who has your back? Draw your squad.

_ _ / _ _ / _ _ _

If you could change anything about the world, what would it be?

_____

_____

_____

_____

_____

_____

_____

_____

_____

_____

_____

_____

_____

_____

_____

_____

_____

How can reading help us feel less alone?

_____

_____

_____

_____

_____

_____

_____

_____

_____

_____

_____

_____

_____

_____

_____

_____

_____

_____

_____

___ / ___ / ___

Time for a check-in! Use this page to describe how you're feeling physically, mentally, and emotionally.

What kinds of stories do you like to read about?

How can people communicate without speaking?

What's something you like to do so much that you could do it for the rest of your life?

_____

_____

_____

_____

_____

_____

_____

_____

_____

_____

_____

_____

_____

_____

_____

_____

_____

_____

_____

_ / _ / _

Goal-setting time! List three new goals and check back when you finish this journal to see your progress.

1 _____
_____
_____
_____
_____

2 _____
_____
_____
_____
_____

3 _____
_____
_____
_____
_____
_____

Finish this sentence! I am powerful because_____.

_____

_____

_____

_____

_____

_____

_____

_____

_____

_____

_____

_____

_____

_____

_____

_____

_____

_____

_____

_____

What are your favorite traits about yourself? Why?

Time for a check-in! **Use this page to describe how you're feeling physically, mentally, and emotionally.**

_____

_____

_____

_____

_____

_____

_____

_____

_____

_____

_____

_____

_____

_____

_____

_____

_____

_____

If you practiced feeling confident every day, what would it look like to you?

_____

_____

_____

_____

_____

_____

_____

_____

_____

_____

_____

_____

_____

_____

_____

_____

_____

_____

Fill in the amount of energy you need to get 100 percent on a test.

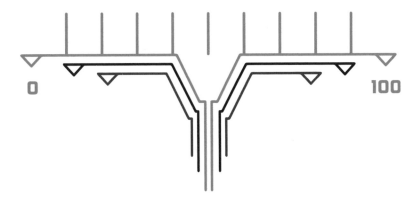

0   100

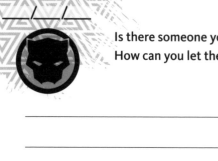

_____ / _____ / _____

Is there someone you wish would treat you differently? How can you let them know?

_____

_____

_____

_____

_____

_____

_____

_____

_____

_____

_____

_____

_____

_____

_____

_____

_____

_____

Wakanda is a technologically advanced nation. If you were the leader of your own nation, how would you use technology to improve people's lives?

_____

_____

_____

_____

_____

_____

_____

_____

_____

_____

_____

_____

_____

_____

_____

_____

_____

_____

___/___/___

Write a thank-you letter to someone you have always wanted to thank. If you want, you can even send the letter!

DEAR _____ ,

_____

_____

_____

_____

_____

_____

_____

_____

_____

_____

_____

_____

_____

_____

FROM _____

Can too much power be a bad thing?

_____ / _____ / _____

___/___/___

Time for a check-in! **Use this page to describe how you're feeling physically, mentally, and emotionally.**

_____

_____

_____

_____

_____

_____

_____

_____

_____

_____

_____

_____

_____

_____

_____

_____

_____

_____

_____

Write about a time when you grew more confident.
How did you do it?

_____ / _____ / _____

_____

_____

_____

_____

_____

_____

_____

_____

_____

_____

_____

_____

_____

_____

_____

_____

_____

_____

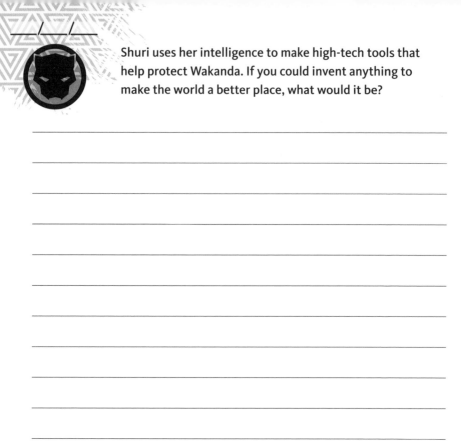

Shuri uses her intelligence to make high-tech tools that help protect Wakanda. If you could invent anything to make the world a better place, what would it be?

List three of your talents and one way you can get better at each of them.

1

2

3

___ / ___ / ___

How can you challenge yourself mentally this week?

_____

_____

_____

_____

_____

_____

_____

_____

_____

_____

_____

_____

_____

_____

_____

_____

_____

_____

_____

_____

How can you challenge yourself physically this week?

___/___/___

Some say laughter is the best medicine. How can laughter heal you?

Time for a check-in! **Use this page to describe how you're feeling physically, mentally, and emotionally.**

_____

_____

_____

_____

_____

_____

_____

_____

_____

_____

_____

_____

_____

_____

_____

_____

_____

_____

_____

_____

___/___/___

In April we celebrate National Super Hero Day. How can you act like a hero today?

_____

_____

_____

_____

_____

_____

_____

_____

_____

_____

_____

_____

_____

_____

_____

_____

_____

_____

What in your world do you want to protect?

_____ / _____ / _____

_____

_____

_____

_____

_____

_____

_____

_____

_____

_____

_____

_____

_____

_____

_____

_____

_____

_____

_____ / _____ / _____

Name three things that make the world beautiful. How can you contribute to that beauty?

1
_____
_____
_____
_____
_____

2
_____
_____
_____
_____
_____

3
_____
_____
_____
_____
_____
_____

A community can be formed by sharing common attitudes, interests, or goals. What attitudes, interests, and goals do you have in common with your community?

_____ / _____ / _____

_____

_____

_____

_____

_____

_____

_____

_____

_____

_____

_____

_____

_____

_____

_____

_____

_____

_____

_____ / _____ / _____

Name five things that you would do if you had an endless supply of courage. How can you make an effort to do at least one of those things today?

1 _____
_____
_____

2 _____
_____
_____

3 _____
_____
_____

4 _____
_____
_____

5 _____
_____
_____
_____

Write a thank-you note to a librarian and tell them why you think libraries are important.

_ / _ / _

DEAR _____ ,

_____

_____

_____

_____

_____

_____

_____

_____

_____

_____

_____

_____

_____

_____

_____

FROM _____

____ / ____ / ____

Time for a check-in! **Use this page to describe how you're feeling physically, mentally, and emotionally.**

_____

_____

_____

_____

_____

_____

_____

_____

_____

_____

_____

_____

_____

_____

_____

_____

_____

_____

Think of someone powerful. What characteristics make them this way?

_ _ / _ _ / _ _ _ _

A team can be a community, but so can family and friends.
List all the communities that you're part of.

What story do you have to tell the world? Why is it important?

_____

_____

_____

_____

_____

_____

_____

_____

_____

_____

_____

_____

_____

_____

_____

_____

_____

_____

_____

Do you need a crown to act like royalty? Why or why not?

___ / ___ / ___

Draw what the world would look like if you made the rules.

_____ / _____ / _____

Goal-setting time! List three new goals for yourself
and check back when you finish this journal to see
your progress.

1 _____
_____
_____
_____
_____

2 _____
_____
_____
_____
_____

3 _____
_____
_____
_____
_____
_____

Time for a check-in! **Use this page to describe how you're feeling physically, mentally, and emotionally.**

_____

_____

_____

_____

_____

_____

_____

_____

_____

_____

_____

_____

_____

_____

_____

_____

_____

_____

_____

_____/_____/_____

Write this phrase seven times below:

"I LOVE MYSELF."

YOU GET TO DECIDE WHAT KIND OF KING YOU ARE GOING TO BE. —Nakia

If you ruled your own nation, describe the kind of leader you would want to be.

_____

_____

_____

_____

_____

_____

_____

_____

_____

_____

_____

_____

_____

_____

_____

_____

____/____/____

When things get tough, what can you say to encourage yourself to keep going? Write as many motivating statements as you can.

_____

_____

_____

_____

_____

_____

_____

_____

_____

_____

_____

_____

_____

_____

_____

_____

_____

_____

T'Challa and Killmonger both want to change the world, but had very different approaches. Finish this sentence: "I will be a change-maker in the world by _____."

___ / ___ / ___

What change would you like to make in your community?
Why?

Think about the most confident person you know. Describe how they show their confidence.

_____

_____

_____

_____

_____

_____

_____

_____

_____

_____

_____

_____

_____

_____

_____

_____

_____

_____

_____ / _____ / _____

Time for a check-in! **Use this page to describe how you're feeling physically, mentally, and emotionally.**

_____

_____

_____

_____

_____

_____

_____

_____

_____

_____

_____

_____

_____

_____

_____

_____

_____

_____

_____

What does sisterhood mean to you?

_____ / _____ / _____

_____

_____

_____

_____

_____

_____

_____

_____

_____

_____

_____

_____

_____

_____

_____

_____

_____

_____

_ _ / _ _ / _ _

What does brotherhood mean to you?

Write about a time when you felt powerful.

___ / ___ / ___

Our friends can help us feel more confident in ourselves.
How do your friends make you feel?

_____

_____

_____

_____

_____

_____

_____

_____

_____

_____

_____

_____

_____

_____

_____

_____

_____

_____

When you are making a decision, whose opinion do you value most? Why?

_____

_____

_____

_____

_____

_____

_____

_____

_____

_____

_____

_____

_____

_____

_____

_____

_____

_____

How can change be good?

_____

_____

_____

_____

_____

_____

_____

_____

_____

_____

_____

_____

_____

_____

_____

_____

_____

_____

_____

_____

_____

Time for a check-in! **Use this page to describe how you're feeling physically, mentally, and emotionally.**

_____

_____

_____

_____

_____

_____

_____

_____

_____

_____

_____

_____

_____

_____

_____

_____

_____

_____

___ / ___ / ___

What can you do to improve someone else's day today?

Reflect on a time when you felt like you belonged.
What did that feel like?

_ / _ / _

Your body is beautiful and unique. Write a letter to your body, thanking it for all it does for you.

DEAR _____ ,

_____

_____

_____

_____

_____

_____

_____

_____

_____

_____

_____

_____

_____

_____

FROM _____

What goals do you have for today? How do you plan to
accomplish them?

_____

_____

_____

_____

_____

_____

_____

_____

_____

_____

_____

_____

_____

_____

_____

_____

_____

_____ / _____ / _____

Write about a time you worked with others to achieve
a goal.

_____

_____

_____

_____

_____

_____

_____

_____

_____

_____

_____

_____

_____

_____

_____

_____

_____

_____

_____

How can different communities come together to change the world for the better?

_____

_____

_____

_____

_____

_____

_____

_____

_____

_____

_____

_____

_____

_____

_____

_____

_____

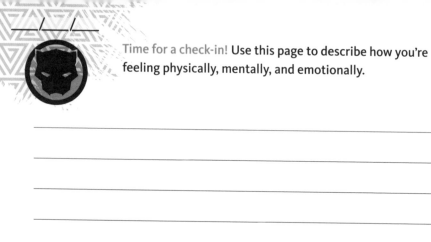

Time for a check-in! Use this page to describe how you're feeling physically, mentally, and emotionally.

"Wakanda Forever" is a phrase that represents Wakandans' loyalty to their nation. Name something that you want to hold close forever. Why is it important to you?

___ / ___ / ___

What is your greatest achievement?

_____

_____

_____

_____

_____

_____

_____

_____

_____

_____

_____

_____

_____

_____

_____

_____

_____

_____

_____

_____

Where do you go to feel safe? Why does this place make you feel safe?

_____ / _____ / _____

_____

_____

_____

_____

_____

_____

_____

_____

_____

_____

_____

_____

_____

_____

_____

_____

_____/_____/_____

Write a thank-you note to your mother or someone who has cared for you like a mother.

DEAR _____ ,

_____

_____

_____

_____

_____

_____

_____

_____

_____

_____

_____

_____

_____

_____

FROM _____

When is the last time you read about a character you admired in a book? Who was the character and why did you find that character admirable?

_____

_____

_____

_____

_____

_____

_____

_____

_____

_____

_____

_____

_____

_____

_____

_____

_____

Write about a time you told the truth, even though it was difficult.

_____ / _____ / _____

Time for a check-in! **Use this page to describe how you're feeling physically, mentally, and emotionally.**

_____

_____

_____

_____

_____

_____

_____

_____

_____

_____

_____

_____

_____

_____

_____

_____

_____

_____

T'Challa says, "In times of crisis the wise build bridges, while the foolish build barriers." Why do you think it's wiser to build bridges than barriers?

_____

_____

_____

_____

_____

_____

_____

_____

_____

_____

_____

_____

_____

_____

_____

_____

Goal-setting time! List three new goals for yourself and check back when you finish this journal to see your progress.

1

_____
_____
_____
_____

2

_____
_____
_____
_____

3

_____
_____
_____
_____
_____

_ _ / _ _ / _ _

Who do you look up to the most? Why?

_____

_____

_____

_____

_____

_____

_____

_____

_____

_____

_____

_____

_____

_____

_____

_____

_____

_____

Write about a time when you felt confident. What will you
do the next time you want to feel confident?

_____

_____

_____

_____

_____

_____

_____

_____

_____

_____

_____

_____

_____

_____

_____

_____

_____

If you had all the money you needed, how would you use it? Why?

Finish this sentence! I will help someone who might need
a friend this week by _____.

_____

_____

_____

_____

_____

_____

_____

_____

_____

_____

_____

_____

_____

_____

_____

_____

_____

_____

___ / ___ / ___

Time for a check-in! **Use this page to describe how you're feeling physically, mentally, and emotionally.**

_____

_____

_____

_____

_____

_____

_____

_____

_____

_____

_____

_____

_____

_____

_____

_____

_____

_____

_____

What characteristics do you have that will make a difference in the world?

_____

_____

_____

_____

_____

_____

_____

_____

_____

_____

_____

_____

_____

_____

_____

_____

_____

_____

_____ / _____ / _____

Write a summary for a book or a movie that hasn't been created yet.

_____

_____

_____

_____

_____

_____

_____

_____

_____

_____

_____

_____

_____

_____

_____

_____

_____

_____

If you were a super hero, what powers would you want?

_____

_____

_____

_____

_____

_____

_____

_____

_____

_____

_____

_____

_____

_____

_____

_____

_____

_____

_ / _ / _

Write about a time that you felt accomplished.

_____

_____

_____

_____

_____

_____

_____

_____

_____

_____

_____

_____

_____

_____

_____

_____

_____

_____

_____

How can you show compassion in your
community this month?

_____ / _____ / _____

_____

_____

_____

_____

_____

_____

_____

_____

_____

_____

_____

_____

_____

_____

_____

_____

_____

_____

_____/_____/_____

What's the bravest thing you've ever done? Describe how it felt.

_____

_____

_____

_____

_____

_____

_____

_____

_____

_____

_____

_____

_____

_____

_____

_____

_____

_____

_____

Time for a check-in! **Use this page to describe how you're feeling physically, mentally, and emotionally.**

_____

_____

_____

_____

_____

_____

_____

_____

_____

_____

_____

_____

_____

_____

_____

_____

_____

_____

If you were a doctor, what illness would you want to help cure? Why?

_____

_____

_____

_____

_____

_____

_____

_____

_____

_____

_____

_____

_____

_____

_____

_____

_____

_____

_____

What do you love about the people you're closest to?
What does that tell you about yourself?

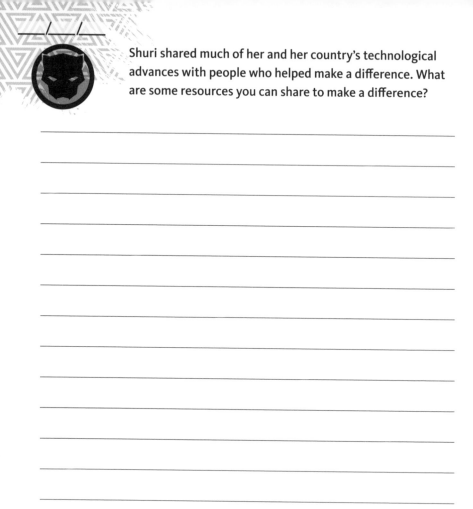

_/_/_

Shuri shared much of her and her country's technological advances with people who helped make a difference. What are some resources you can share to make a difference?

_____

_____

_____

_____

_____

_____

_____

_____

_____

_____

_____

_____

_____

_____

_____

_____

_____

Practice striking a pose that makes you feel confident.
Look at yourself in the mirror and draw or describe the pose.
Try this the next time you feel nervous.

___/___/___

Think of five things you love doing. Try to do one of them
the next time you're feeling stressed or overwhelmed.

1

2

3

4

5

How can being prepared help you feel less nervous?

___/___/___

Time for a check-in! **Use this page to describe how you're feeling physically, mentally, and emotionally.**

What values are important to you and your community?

__ / __ / __

Why is it important to back up your words with actions?

The Dora Milaje are warrior women who help protect the kingdom of Wakanda. What women in your life are warriors?

_____

_____

_____

_____

_____

_____

_____

_____

_____

_____

_____

_____

_____

_____

_____

_____

_____

___ / ___ / ___

Drinking water throughout the day energizes your body so that you can think and perform your best. What other healthy habits could you form to help you accomplish your goals today?

_____

_____

_____

_____

_____

_____

_____

_____

_____

_____

_____

_____

_____

_____

_____

Sometimes, learning a new skill helps you feel empowered. Name three new skills that you'd like to learn and why they're important to you.

1. _____

_____

_____

_____

2. _____

_____

_____

_____

3. _____

_____

_____

_____

_____

___ / ___ / ___

How can you show strength without being physically strong?

Time for a check-in! **Use this page to describe how you're feeling physically, mentally, and emotionally.**

_____

_____

_____

_____

_____

_____

_____

_____

_____

_____

_____

_____

_____

_____

_____

_____

_____

_____

_____ / ___ / ___

What animal most represents strength? Why? Draw it!

How can communities look out for each other?

_____/_____/_____

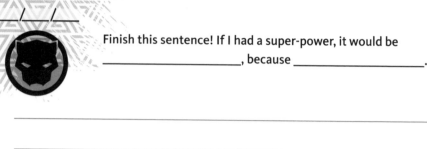

_ _ / _ _ / _ _

Finish this sentence! If I had a super-power, it would be
_____, because _____.

_____

_____

_____

_____

_____

_____

_____

_____

_____

_____

_____

_____

_____

_____

_____

_____

_____

_____

_____

_____

Success looks different for everyone. What does success
mean to you?

_____

_____

_____

_____

_____

_____

_____

_____

_____

_____

_____

_____

_____

_____

_____

_____

_____

_ _ / _ _ / _ _

Goal-setting time! List three new goals and check back when you finish this journal to see your progress.

1 _____

_____

_____

_____

_____

2 _____

_____

_____

_____

_____

3 _____

_____

_____

_____

_____

Breathe in Power! Breathe in through your nose while writing 1, 2, 3, and 4 on this page. Now breathe out through your mouth while writing 1, 2, 3, 4, 5, 6, 7, 8. Repeat four times.

___ / ___ / ___

Time for a check-in! **Use this page to describe how you're feeling physically, mentally, and emotionally.**

Name a leader in your community. Which skills helped them get there?

_____

_____

_____

_____

_____

_____

_____

_____

_____

_____

_____

_____

_____

_____

_____

_____

_____ / _____ / _____

List someone who changed the world for the better in the past and someone changing the world for the better now.

_____
_____
_____
_____
_____
_____
_____
_____
_____
_____
_____
_____
_____
_____
_____
_____
_____
_____
_____
_____
_____
_____

Who's the Okoye to your Black Panther? Draw a picture of your most loyal friend!

___/___/___

List four qualities of a great leader.

1

_____

_____

_____

_____

2

_____

_____

_____

_____

3

_____

_____

_____

_____

4

_____

_____

_____

_____

How can you show up as the best version of yourself today?
Be specific.

_____ / _____ / _____

_____

_____

_____

_____

_____

_____

_____

_____

_____

_____

_____

_____

_____

_____

_____

_____

_ / _ / _

How can sharing what we have with our community make the world better?

_____

_____

_____

_____

_____

_____

_____

_____

_____

_____

_____

_____

_____

_____

_____

_____

_____

_____

Time for a check-in! **Use this page to describe how you're feeling physically, mentally, and emotionally.**

_____ / _____ / _____

_____

_____

_____

_____

_____

_____

_____

_____

_____

_____

_____

_____

_____

_____

_____

_____

_____

_____

What do you need to learn to change the world the way you want to?

_____

_____

_____

_____

_____

_____

_____

_____

_____

_____

_____

_____

_____

_____

_____

_____

_____

_____

How can curiosity be a gift?

How is your community a reflection of yourself?

Black Panther's suit is made from vibranium, a rare resource. Choose three of your own resources that you'd like to stitch into the fabric of your day.

KINDNESS

CALMNESS

CONFIDENCE

ENERGY

CREATIVITY

INTELLIGENCE

FUN

UNDERSTANDING

_ _ / _ _ / _ _

What's the best advice you've ever heard? Who gave you
this advice and when did they give it to you?

Wakanda has many shops and markets. If you were queen
or king, what kind of businesses would you want in your city?

_____

_____

_____

_____

_____

_____

_____

_____

_____

_____

_____

_____

_____

_____

_____

_____

_____

_____ / _____ / _____

List three things that made you feel proud this week.

1

_____

_____

_____

_____

2

_____

_____

_____

_____

3

_____

_____

_____

_____

_____

Time for a check-in! **Use this page to describe how you're feeling physically, mentally, and emotionally.**

_____

_____

_____

_____

_____

_____

_____

_____

_____

_____

_____

_____

_____

_____

_____

_____

_____

_____/_____/_____

What's one way to cheer yourself up when you're feeling down?

_____

_____

_____

_____

_____

_____

_____

_____

_____

_____

_____

_____

_____

_____

_____

_____

_____

_____

Which of your friends do you trust the most? Why?

_ _ / _ _ / _ _

REPRESENTATION IS SOMETHING THAT CAN BE VERY POWERFUL. —*Ryan Coogler*, Black Panther *director*

Why do you think representation is important?

Describe the last time you felt joyful, happy, and free.

_____/_____/_____

__/__/__

The Black Panther has a suit that expresses their power.
How can an outfit make you feel powerful?

_____

_____

_____

_____

_____

_____

_____

_____

_____

_____

_____

_____

_____

_____

_____

Time for a check-in! **Use this page to describe how you're feeling physically, mentally, and emotionally.**

_____

_____

_____

_____

_____

_____

_____

_____

_____

_____

_____

_____

_____

_____

_____

___ / ___ / ___

What will you work on getting better at tomorrow?

Okoye fiercely and unapologetically protects Wakanda, her home. In what ways can you protect your home?

___ / ___ / ___

What is your favorite hairstyle or hair accessory, and how does it make you feel?

_____

_____

_____

_____

_____

_____

_____

_____

_____

_____

_____

_____

_____

_____

_____

_____

_____

_____

I'VE SEEN TOO MANY IN NEED JUST TO TURN A BLIND EYE. I CAN'T BE HAPPY HERE KNOWING THAT THERE'S PEOPLE OUT THERE WHO HAVE NOTHING. —Nakia to T'Challa in Black Panther

What are some small things you can do to help those outside of your community?

_____

_____

_____

_____

_____

_____

_____

_____

_____

_____

_____

_____

_____

Is there anyone you wish you could talk to right now? Draw something that reminds you of them, and write them a note.

If you could ask world leaders to change anything, what would you ask them to do?

_____

_____

_____

_____

_____

_____

_____

_____

_____

_____

_____

_____

_____

_____

_____

_____

_____

_____

_____

___ / ___ / ___

Time for a check-in! **Use this page to describe how you're feeling physically, mentally, and emotionally.**

What colors represent power to you? Draw yourself
wearing those colors!

___/___/___

Goal-setting time! List three new goals and check back when you finish this journal to see your progress.

1
_____
_____
_____
_____

2
_____
_____
_____
_____

3
_____
_____
_____
_____

If you wrote a song or a rap about being powerful, what would the title be? Why?

_____

_____

_____

_____

_____

_____

_____

_____

_____

_____

_____

_____

_____

_____

_____

_____

_____

_____

_____ / _____ / _____

Reflect on a time when you made a mistake. What lesson did you learn from the mistake and what will you do differently next time?

_____

_____

_____

_____

_____

_____

_____

_____

_____

_____

_____

_____

_____

_____

_____

_____

_____

Can a community be made up of just two people? Why or why not?

_____

_____

_____

_____

_____

_____

_____

_____

_____

_____

_____

_____

_____

_____

_____

_____

_____

_____

_____

_____/_____/_____

Wakanda protects itself and its people from outsiders with a tech-created facade. Name a place or a person in your community that you want to protect.

_____

_____

_____

_____

_____

_____

_____

_____

_____

_____

_____

_____

_____

_____

_____

_____

_____

Time for a check-in! **Use this page to describe how you're feeling physically, mentally, and emotionally.**

___ / ___ / ___

_____

_____

_____

_____

_____

_____

_____

_____

_____

_____

_____

_____

_____

_____

_____

_____

_____

_____

___/___/___

Write about a time when you felt mentally or physically strong.

How can the past affect the present?

_ _ / _ _ / _ _

___ / __ / __

How can the present affect the future?

Everything possible now was once thought to be impossible.
What impossible thing would you like to help make possible?

___/___/___

What's your dream career? Why?

Finish this sentence! People say that being strong means
_____, but I really think that being strong
means _____.

_____

_____

_____

_____

_____

_____

_____

_____

_____

_____

_____

_____

_____

_____

_____

_____

_____

_____

_ _ / _ _ / _ _

Time for a check-in! **Use this page to describe how you're feeling physically, mentally, and emotionally.**

_____

_____

_____

_____

_____

_____

_____

_____

_____

_____

_____

_____

_____

_____

_____

_____

_____

_____

Describe the relationship between knowledge and power.

T'Challa looks out for people who have been treated unfairly. Do you know of anyone who gets treated unfairly? How can you help?

_____

_____

_____

_____

_____

_____

_____

_____

_____

_____

_____

_____

_____

_____

_____

How can you show confidence without bragging?

_ _ / _ _ / _ _

Write about a time when you experienced change.

___/___/___

Draw a symbol that represents strength. Describe why this symbol is strong.

Write about a time someone helped you, and it changed your day for the better. Pay it forward by helping someone else today.

_____

_____

_____

_____

_____

_____

_____

_____

_____

_____

_____

_____

_____

_____

_____

_____

_____

Time for a check-in! **Use this page to describe how you're feeling physically, mentally, and emotionally.**

_____

_____

_____

_____

_____

_____

_____

_____

_____

_____

_____

_____

_____

_____

_____

_____

___/___/___

Do you think it's important for role models to be kind? Why or why not?

Reflect: Can you be in community with animals, objects, places, or things? Explain why or why not.

_____/_____/_____

_____

_____

_____

_____

_____

_____

_____

_____

_____

_____

_____

_____

_____

_____

_____

_____

Phillis Wheatley was only 12 years old when she published her first poem in 1773. What dream can you work toward today, regardless of your age?

_____

_____

_____

_____

_____

_____

_____

_____

_____

_____

_____

_____

_____

_____

_____

_____

_____

_____

Black Panther teaches us that both elderly and young people are valuable. Describe how both are important to you and your community.

_____

_____

_____

_____

_____

_____

_____

_____

_____

_____

_____

_____

_____

_____

_____

_____

_____

_ _ / _ _ / _ _

Finish this sentence! Everyone deserves_____.

Create an imaginary place where it's safe and you feel peaceful. Draw this place, and describe why you chose it.

_ _/_ _/_ _

Time for a check-in! Use this page to describe how you're feeling physically, mentally, and emotionally.

_____

_____

_____

_____

_____

_____

_____

_____

_____

_____

_____

_____

_____

_____

_____

_____

_____

_____

_____

Power comes with responsibility. What responsibilities do you have?

What's a small problem in your school or neighborhood that you can help fix?

_____

_____

_____

_____

_____

_____

_____

_____

_____

_____

_____

_____

_____

_____

_____

Write about the last time you felt like a leader.

_ / _ / _

Strength comes from surprising places. Iron, steel, and metal are known to be strong, but think of another material you might not expect to be strong. Write about what makes that material strong.

_____

_____

_____

_____

_____

_____

_____

_____

_____

_____

_____

_____

_____

_____

_____

Goal-setting time! List three new goals for yourself and check back when you finish this journal to see your progress.

___ / ___ / ___

1

_____
_____
_____
_____

2

_____
_____
_____
_____

3

_____
_____
_____
_____
_____

___ / ___ / ___

Take a moment to relax. Sit in silence, close your eyes, and count to 30. Slowly take deep breaths in and out. Open your eyes and write down whatever you're thinking about.

Time for a check-in! Use this page to describe how you're feeling physically, mentally, and emotionally.

_____

_____

_____

_____

_____

_____

_____

_____

_____

_____

_____

_____

_____

_____

_____

_____

_____

_____

_____ / _____ / _____

Clear communication helps build strong communities. What's something that you've always wanted to say to someone you care about?

_____

_____

_____

_____

_____

_____

_____

_____

_____

_____

_____

_____

_____

_____

_____

_____

_____

_____

What's the name of your favorite *Black Panther* actor or actress? Why are they your favorite?

_____

_____

_____

_____

_____

_____

_____

_____

_____

_____

_____

_____

_____

_____

_____

_____

_____

_____

Courage takes practice. How can you practice being brave today?

_____

_____

_____

_____

_____

_____

_____

_____

_____

_____

_____

_____

_____

_____

_____

_____

_____

_____

Our hair is our crown! Write a love letter to your hair.

How can your attitude affect your goals?

If you wrote a book about your life, what would the title be?

_____ / _____ / _____

Time for a check-in! **Use this page to describe how you're feeling physically, mentally, and emotionally.**

_____

_____

_____

_____

_____

_____

_____

_____

_____

_____

_____

_____

_____

_____

_____

_____

_____

_____

_____

Describe why it's important to spend time with yourself and how it might positively influence the time you spend with other people.

_____

_____

_____

_____

_____

_____

_____

_____

_____

_____

_____

_____

_____

_____

_____

_____

_____

_ _ / _ _ / _ _

Name a hero who doesn't have super-powers. What makes them a hero?

We all have something to teach someone else. Do you prefer communicating through words or actions? Why?

_____ / _____ / _____

_____

_____

_____

_____

_____

_____

_____

_____

_____

_____

_____

_____

_____

_____

_____

_____

_____

_____ / _____ / _____

List five things that help you stay calm.

1

2

3

4

5

Circle all that apply: I am strong because _____.

A. I STAND UP FOR MYSELF.

B. I STAND UP FOR OTHERS.

C. I SPEAK UP WHEN IT'S HARD.

D. I AM NOT AFRAID TO BE MYSELF.

E. I AM NOT AFRAID TO MAKE MISTAKES.

F. I AM NOT AFRAID TO BE VULNERABLE
BY SHOWING MY EMOTIONS.

Black Panther shows how a community stays strong by valuing each of its members. How else does a community stay strong?

_____

_____

_____

_____

_____

_____

_____

_____

_____

_____

_____

_____

_____

_____

_____

_____

_____

_____

Time for a check-in! **Use this page to describe how you're feeling physically, mentally, and emotionally.**

____ / ____ / ____

_____

_____

_____

_____

_____

_____

_____

_____

_____

_____

_____

_____

_____

_____

_____

_____

_____

_____

_____ / _____ / _____

Finish this sentence! Even though I sometimes doubt myself, my confidence comes from _____.

Sometimes when you lose something, you can gain something better. Has this ever happened to you? If so, describe a time when this happened to you.

_____

_____

_____

_____

_____

_____

_____

_____

_____

_____

_____

_____

_____

_____

_____

_____

_____

Why is it important for people to see themselves represented on-screen or in the pages of a book?

_____

_____

_____

_____

_____

_____

_____

_____

_____

_____

_____

_____

_____

_____

_____

_____

_____

_____

How can you show people you care about them without
spending money?

_____

_____

_____

_____

_____

_____

_____

_____

_____

_____

_____

_____

_____

_____

_____

_____

_____

How can working together with a group help you achieve a goal? How is it different from working alone?

_____

_____

_____

_____

_____

_____

_____

_____

_____

_____

_____

_____

_____

_____

_____

_____

_____

Draw a picture of what you'll look like in 10 years! Write about what you can do now to become the person you want to be.

___ / ___ / ___

___/___/___

Time for a check-in! **Use this page to describe how you're feeling physically, mentally, and emotionally.**

In your opinion, what's the strongest part of your body? Why?

_ _ / _ _ / _ _

Write about a time when you had to work up the courage to do something. How did that make you feel?

_____

_____

_____

_____

_____

_____

_____

_____

_____

_____

_____

_____

_____

_____

_____

_____

_____

_____

_____

Wakanda is a kingdom, which means that the crown can be passed down from generation to generation. What is something that has been passed down in your family? It could be a talent, an idea, a tradition, or something else.

_____

_____

_____

_____

_____

_____

_____

_____

_____

_____

_____

_____

_____

_____

_____

_____

_ _ / _ _ / _ _

Ants may be small, but they are mighty. They can lift as much as 50 times their weight. Has anyone ever doubted what you can do? How did you prove them wrong?

_____

_____

_____

_____

_____

_____

_____

_____

_____

_____

_____

_____

_____

_____

_____

_____

_____

_____

When you disagree with someone, what questions can you
ask to better understand their point of view?

_____

_____

_____

_____

_____

_____

_____

_____

_____

_____

_____

_____

_____

_____

_____

_____

_____

How can you use what you have to help other people?

_____

_____

_____

_____

_____

_____

_____

_____

_____

_____

_____

_____

_____

_____

_____

_____

_____

_____

Time for a check-in! **Use this page to describe how you're feeling physically, mentally, and emotionally.**

_ / _ / _

Goal-setting time! List three new goals and check back
when you finish this journal to see your progress.

1 _____
_____
_____
_____
_____

2 _____
_____
_____
_____

3 _____
_____
_____
_____
_____

If you were a community leader, what would be your first plan of action? Why?

_____

_____

_____

_____

_____

_____

_____

_____

_____

_____

_____

_____

_____

_____

_____

_____

Research an Afro-Latino person in history. What did you learn about courage from their life story?

_____

_____

_____

_____

_____

_____

_____

_____

_____

_____

_____

_____

_____

_____

_____

_____

_____

Give an example of someone using their power to give power to others.

_____ / _____ / _____

_____

_____

_____

_____

_____

_____

_____

_____

_____

_____

_____

_____

_____

_____

_____

_____

_____

_____

___ / __ / __

How did you show strength today?

Brainstorm three ways to help out at home.

1

2

3

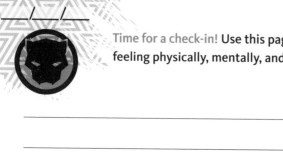

____/____/____

Time for a check-in! **Use this page to describe how you're feeling physically, mentally, and emotionally.**

_____
_____
_____
_____
_____
_____
_____
_____
_____
_____
_____
_____
_____
_____
_____
_____
_____
_____

The women warriors of the Dora Milaje are loyal to the country of Wakanda, which they fiercely serve by protecting it. What is worthy of your loyalty, and how do you show it?

_____

_____

_____

_____

_____

_____

_____

_____

_____

_____

_____

_____

_____

_____

_____

_____

_____

___ / ___ / ___

How would you describe the people and places in your neighborhood to someone who has never visited there?

_____

_____

_____

_____

_____

_____

_____

_____

_____

_____

_____

_____

_____

_____

_____

_____

_____

_____

Finish this sentence! I am proud of myself for _____ **and** _____.

_____

_____

_____

_____

_____

_____

_____

_____

_____

_____

_____

_____

_____

_____

_____

_____

_____

_____

_____

If you could ask any character in *Black Panther* a question, who would it be and what would you ask?

How can you show that your heart is strong?

_____

_____

_____

_____

_____

_____

_____

_____

_____

_____

_____

_____

_____

_____

_____

_____

_____

Time for a check-in! **Use this page to describe how you're feeling physically, mentally, and emotionally.**

How can love lead to positive change in the world?

_ / _ / _

Write about a time when you saw an example of
good leadership. What qualities made this person
a good leader?

_____

_____

_____

_____

_____

_____

_____

_____

_____

_____

_____

_____

_____

_____

_____

_____

_____

_____

Do you think people in the same community can have different opinions? Why or why not?

_____/_____/_____

_____

_____

_____

_____

_____

_____

_____

_____

_____

_____

_____

_____

_____

_____

_____

_____

_____

_ / _ / _

The Heart-Shaped Herb is a plant native to Wakanda that gives the Black Panther enhanced powers. What foods fuel you up and give you energy for the day?

_____

_____

_____

_____

_____

_____

_____

_____

_____

_____

_____

_____

_____

_____

_____

_____

_____

Research a Black historical figure. What did you learn about them?

_____

_____

_____

_____

_____

_____

_____

_____

_____

_____

_____

_____

_____

_____

_____

_____

_____

_____/_____/_____

Draw a symbol that represents who you are to the world.
Explain the meaning of this symbol.

Time for a check-in! **Use this page to describe how you're feeling physically, mentally, and emotionally.**

_____

_____

_____

_____

_____

_____

_____

_____

_____

_____

_____

_____

_____

_____

_____

_____ / _____ / _____

Write a thank-you note to someone you look up to.

DEAR _____ ,

_____

_____

_____

_____

_____

_____

_____

_____

_____

_____

_____

_____

_____

FROM _____

Queen Nefertiti ruled beside her husband, and some say that she became king after her husband's death. Describe the traits of someone you'd like to rule beside.

_____

_____

_____

_____

_____

_____

_____

_____

_____

_____

_____

_____

_____

_____

_____

_____

_____

_____

Name a young person changing the world today.
How do they inspire you?

_____

_____

_____

_____

_____

_____

_____

_____

_____

_____

_____

_____

_____

_____

_____

_____

_____

_____

What animal do you think of when you hear the word power?
Why?

_____ / _____ / _____

_____

_____

_____

_____

_____

_____

_____

_____

_____

_____

_____

_____

_____

_____

_____

_____

_____

Take a deep breath. How does your body feel?
Describe it here.

_____

_____

_____

_____

_____

_____

_____

_____

_____

_____

_____

_____

_____

_____

_____

_____

_____

_____

_____

If you could learn any language in the world, which one would you learn? Why?

___ / ___ / ___

Time for a check-in! **Use this page to describe how you're feeling physically, mentally, and emotionally.**

How can you grow stronger from winning?

_ _ / _ _ / _ _

___/___/___

How can losing make you stronger?

_____

_____

_____

_____

_____

_____

_____

_____

_____

_____

_____

_____

_____

_____

_____

_____

_____

_____

_____

Can you think of a time when your actions affected others?
Describe what happened.

___ / ___ / ___

_____

_____

_____

_____

_____

_____

_____

_____

_____

_____

_____

_____

_____

_____

_____

_____

_____

_____

_____

_ / _ / _

List five organizations that are making your community a better place. Find at least two events or fundraisers by those organizations that you'd like to help out with. How would you like to help?

1

2

3

4

5

How do you show you care about other people in your community?

_____ / _____ / _____

___ / ___ / ___

Goal-setting time! List three new goals and check back when you finish this journal to see your progress.

1 _____

_____

_____

_____

2 _____

_____

_____

_____

3 _____

_____

_____

_____

_____

Time for a check-in! **Use this page to describe how you're feeling physically, mentally, and emotionally.**

_____

_____

_____

_____

_____

_____

_____

_____

_____

_____

_____

_____

_____

_____

_____

_____

_____

_____

_____

How do you like to relax when you've had a busy day?

Finish this sentence! Even if everyone else lets me down,
I can always depend on myself to _____.

_____ / _____ / _____

_____

_____

_____

_____

_____

_____

_____

_____

_____

_____

_____

_____

_____

_____

_____

_____

_____

_____

_ _ / _ _ / _ _ _ _

Vibranium, a rare and powerful metal, is a source of power and pride for all Wakandans. What parts of your country or community make you proud?

_____

_____

_____

_____

_____

_____

_____

_____

_____

_____

_____

_____

_____

_____

_____

_____

_____

_____

_____

_____

_____

What qualities make a great leader? Why?

___ / ___ / ___

_ _ / _ _ / _ _ _ _

Write about a time when you accomplished a goal.
How did that feel?

_____

_____

_____

_____

_____

_____

_____

_____

_____

_____

_____

_____

_____

_____

_____

_____

_____

_____

Who are the kindest people in your community, and how do they show their kindness?

_____

_____

_____

_____

_____

_____

_____

_____

_____

_____

_____

_____

_____

_____

_____

_____

_____

_____

__/__/__

Time for a check-in! **Use this page to describe how you're feeling physically, mentally, and emotionally.**

_____

_____

_____

_____

_____

_____

_____

_____

_____

_____

_____

_____

_____

_____

_____

_____

_____

_____

_____

How can the truth be powerful?

___ / ___ / ___

What small actions could help make the world a better place?

Name a character from a book who reminds you of yourself.
How are they similar to you?

___/___/___

Describe how music, words, or art can be powerful.

Think of a need that your community has. How can you
help meet that need?

_____

_____

_____

_____

_____

_____

_____

_____

_____

_____

_____

_____

_____

_____

_____

_____

_____

_____/_____/_____

If you ran a nation, what services would you offer free of charge for your people, and why?

Time for a check-in! **Use this page to describe how you're feeling physically, mentally, and emotionally.**

_____

_____

_____

_____

_____

_____

_____

_____

_____

_____

_____

_____

_____

_____

_____

_____

_____

_____

Sometimes facing our fears pays off. Draw a monster, and write down one fear inside it. At the top of the page, write "I can handle it."

What colors help you feel calm? Draw a peaceful scene
using those colors.

Why is love powerful?

You can decide how you want to respond to challenges in
your life. Do you want to be calm, brave, hopeful, or curious?

_____

_____

_____

_____

_____

_____

_____

_____

_____

_____

_____

_____

_____

_____

_____

_____

_____

_ _ / _ _ / _ _

Draw a picture of yourself in five years! What goals will you have then?

Finish this sentence! I've learned to _____ this year, so I will celebrate by _____.

_____

_____

_____

_____

_____

_____

_____

_____

_____

_____

_____

_____

_____

_____

_____

_____

_____

_____

___ / ___ / ___

Time for a check-in! **Use this page to describe how you're feeling physically, mentally, and emotionally.**

What do you think it means to be a warrior?

_ _ / _ _ / _ _

In what ways can you form community with others?

Okoye says that Killmonger is not fit to be king because he has hatred in his heart. Why is it important for rulers to lead with compassion?

What lessons can we learn from plants that grow through the sidewalk?

_____

_____

_____

_____

_____

_____

_____

_____

_____

_____

_____

_____

_____

_____

_____

_____

_____

_____

Write about a time when you had a lot of fun.

_____ / _____ / _____

Goal-setting time! List three new goals and check back when you finish this journal to see your progress.

1
_____
_____
_____
_____

2
_____
_____
_____

3
_____
_____
_____
_____

Time for a check-in! **Use this page to describe how you're feeling physically, mentally, and emotionally.**

_____

_____

_____

_____

_____

_____

_____

_____

_____

_____

_____

_____

_____

_____

_____

_____

_____

_____

_____

_ _ / _ _ / _ _

Do you think you can change the world by being more loving? Why or why not?

_____

_____

_____

_____

_____

_____

_____

_____

_____

_____

_____

_____

_____

_____

_____

_____

Sometimes writing a letter can help you express your
emotions, even if you never send it. Write a letter to
someone in your community who has hurt you.

_____ / _____ / _____

DEAR _____ ,

_____

_____

_____

_____

_____

_____

_____

_____

_____

_____

_____

_____

_____

_____

_____

FROM _____

___ / ___ / ___

Can change be bad?

_____

_____

_____

_____

_____

_____

_____

_____

_____

_____

_____

_____

_____

_____

_____

_____

_____

_____

_____

How can books heal us?

_ _/_ _/_ _

Doubt can trick you into believing that you can't do something, even if it's not true. Has that ever happened to you? Write about that experience.

_____

_____

_____

_____

_____

_____

_____

_____

_____

_____

_____

_____

_____

_____

_____

_____

_____

_____

Time for a check-in! **Use this page to describe how you're feeling physically, mentally, and emotionally.**

_____

_____

_____

_____

_____

_____

_____

_____

_____

_____

_____

_____

_____

_____

_____

_____

_____

_____

_____

_____

_____ / _____ / _____

Write about a time when you overcame doubt.
How did you do it?

_____

_____

_____

_____

_____

_____

_____

_____

_____

_____

_____

_____

_____

_____

_____

_____

_____

_____

_____

How can your community help you achieve your goals?

_ _/_ _/_ _

How can thinking of things you're thankful for help you find peace?

_____

_____

_____

_____

_____

_____

_____

_____

_____

_____

_____

_____

_____

_____

_____

_____

Power comes with responsibility. What power would you like to have? Why?

_____

_____

_____

_____

_____

_____

_____

_____

_____

_____

_____

_____

_____

_____

_____

_____

_____

_____

_____

How are peace and justice related?

What does being a good role model mean?

____ / ____ / ____

Time for a check-in! **Use this page to describe how you're feeling physically, mentally, and emotionally.**

If you could create a nation like Wakanda, what would its leading principles be?

_____

_____

_____

_____

_____

_____

_____

_____

_____

_____

_____

_____

_____

_____

_____

_____

_____

_____

Do you prefer working by yourself or with a team? How can you get better at both?

_____

_____

_____

_____

_____

_____

_____

_____

_____

_____

_____

_____

_____

_____

_____

_____

_____

Make an emergency plan for when you feel tired, frustrated, or scared.

_____

_____

_____

_____

_____

_____

_____

_____

_____

_____

_____

_____

_____

_____

_____

_____

_____

_____

_____

_____

___ / ___ / ___

How can you practice treating yourself well?

Finish this sentence! I know myself best because _____.

_____

_____

_____

_____

_____

_____

_____

_____

_____

_____

_____

_____

_____

_____

_____

_____

_____

___/___/___

Shuri believes that there's always room for improvement. What do you wish to improve in your life? How do you plan to work on that?

_____

_____

_____

_____

_____

_____

_____

_____

_____

_____

_____

_____

_____

_____

_____

_____

_____

_____

Time for a check-in! **Use this page to describe how you're feeling physically, mentally, and emotionally.**

_ _ / _ _ / _ _

_____

_____

_____

_____

_____

_____

_____

_____

_____

_____

_____

_____

_____

_____

_____

_____

_____

Draw an outfit that makes you feel confident.

What does it mean to have a "lion's heart"?

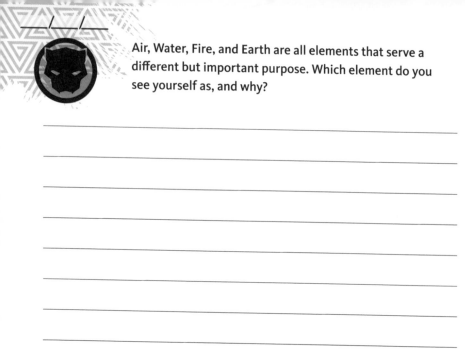

Air, Water, Fire, and Earth are all elements that serve a different but important purpose. Which element do you see yourself as, and why?

What's your vibranium? Think of a gem that most represents you and why.

Examples: diamond, gold, silver, emerald, ruby, onyx

_____

_____

_____

_____

_____

_____

_____

_____

_____

_____

_____

_____

_____

_____

_____

_____

_____

_____

How can reading help us create a better world?

_____

_____

_____

_____

_____

_____

_____

_____

_____

_____

_____

_____

_____

_____

_____

_____

_____

_____

_____

Goal-setting time! List three new goals for yourself and check back when you finish this journal to see your progress.

_____ / _____ / _____

1
_____
_____
_____
_____
_____

2
_____
_____
_____
_____
_____

3
_____
_____
_____
_____
_____

___ / ___ / ___

Time for a check-in! **Use this page to describe how you're feeling physically, mentally, and emotionally.**

Finish this sentence! Some people think that because turtles move slowly, they are weak; but a strength turtles have is _____.

_____

_____

_____

_____

_____

_____

_____

_____

_____

_____

_____

_____

_____

_____

_____

_____

_____

_____

_____

What are some reasons that a person might try to build a community?

What's one way you can conquer your fears?

Why is listening an important skill for strong leaders to have?

_____

_____

_____

_____

_____

_____

_____

_____

_____

_____

_____

_____

_____

_____

_____

_____

_____

Imagine yourself in five years. Describe who you are, what you like to do, and something that makes you proud of your future self.

_____

_____

_____

_____

_____

_____

_____

_____

_____

_____

_____

_____

_____

_____

_____

_____

_____

How can you practice feeling confident in yourself, even if others doubt you?

_____

_____

_____

_____

_____

_____

_____

_____

_____

_____

_____

_____

_____

_____

_____

Time for a check-in! Use this page to describe how you're feeling physically, mentally, and emotionally.

_____ / _____ / _____

_____

_____

_____

_____

_____

_____

_____

_____

_____

_____

_____

_____

_____

_____

_____

_____

_____

_____

_____

_____

Describe what you think the future should look like for your community and the larger world.

If you could choose a place to be the next wonder of the world, where would it be, and why?

_____

_____

_____

_____

_____

_____

_____

_____

_____

_____

_____

_____

_____

_____

_____

_____

_____

_____

Kwanzaa is a celebration of African-American community, family, and culture. Some of its principles are *Umoja* (unity), *Nia* (purpose), *Kuumba* (creativity), and *Imani* (faith). Choose one of these principles and write about what it means to you.

_____

_____

_____

_____

_____

_____

_____

_____

_____

_____

_____

_____

_____

_____

_____

_____

_____

_____

What skills could you use to make the world a better place?

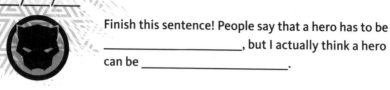

Finish this sentence! People say that a hero has to be
_____, but I actually think a hero
can be _____.

_____

_____

_____

_____

_____

_____

_____

_____

_____

_____

_____

_____

_____

_____

_____

_____

_____

Write a poem about finding your power.

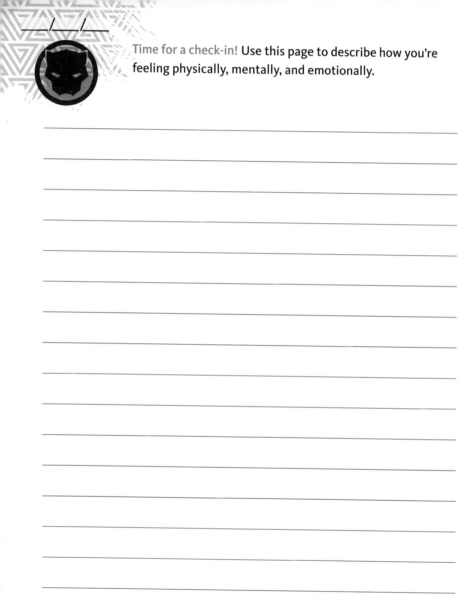

_ _ / _ _ / _ _

Time for a check-in! **Use this page to describe how you're feeling physically, mentally, and emotionally.**

Write a hype-up plan for when you get scared or doubt yourself.

_____ / _____ / _____

___ / ___ / ___

Look back at the goals you set for yourself this year.
How much progress did you make?

_____

_____

_____

_____

_____

_____

_____

_____

_____

_____

_____

_____

_____

_____

_____

_____

_____

_____

_____